100 SNOWMEN

By **Jen Arena**   Illustrated by **Stephen Gilpin**

two lions

two lions

Amazon Publishing
Attn: Amazon Children's Publishing
P.O. Box 400818
Las Vegas, NV 89140
www.amazon.com/amazonchildrenspublishing

Library of Congress Cataloging-in-Publication Data is available upon request.

ISBN-13: 9781477847039 (hardcover)
ISBN-10: 1477847030 (hardcover)
ISBN-13: 9781477897034 (eBook)
ISBN-10: B00C7XTOQY (eBook)

Book design by Katrina Damkoehler
Editor: Margery Cuyler

Printed in China (R)
First edition
10 9 8 7 6 5 4 3 2 1

For Mac and Ailyn
—J.A.

For Angie. You're my beautiful little snowflake.
—S.G.

One lonely snowman has a carrot nose.

Two other snowmen join him when it snows.
1+2=3

Three more snowmen count the stars at night.

Four more snowmen have a snowball fight.
3+4=7

Five more snowmen
sledding down the hill.

Six more snowmen never catch a chill.
5+6=11

Seven more snowmen
make a snowshoe track.
Eight more snowmen
build a fort in back.
7+8=15

Nine more snowmen
skip and laugh and play.

Ten more snowmen
run the other way!
9+10=19

Nine more snowmen
like to have a race.

Eight more snowmen make a funny face. 9+8=17

Seven more snowmen try on hats and mittens.

Six more snowmen find a bunch of kittens!
7+6=13

Five more snowmen
skate on silver ice.

Four more snowmen
think cold water's nice!
5+4=9

Three more snowmen
playing hide-and-seek.

Two more snowmen
trying not to peek.
$3+2=5$

One last snowman calls out to his friends,
then . . .
every single snowman wants to play again!
1+2+3+4+5+6+7+8+9+10+9+
8+7+6+5+4+3+2+1=100